Kitten
in Trouble

by Maria Polushkin · pictures by Betsy Lewin

Bradbury Press · New York

10   9   8   7   6   5   4   3   2   1

The text of this book is set in ITC Caslon No. 224 Book.

Library of Congress Cataloging in Publication Data

Polushkin, Maria.
Kitten in trouble.

Summary: A kitten wakes up early
and decides to explore the house.
1. Children's stories, American.
[1. Cats—Fiction]
I. Lewin, Betsy, ill.
II. Title.
PZ7.P7695Ki   1988   [E]   85-5753
ISBN 0-02-774740-9

Kitten wakes up early
and wants to play.

He sees two feet,
ten little toes.
The toes wiggle...

Kitten pounces.

Oh-oh.

Kitten's in trouble!

Kitten chases a ball.

He sees a basket
filled with roly-poly
balls of yarn.

Kitten smells bacon frying.

Kitten's in trouble!

Oh-oh.

Kitten pounces.

He sees some eggs,

he sees some milk.

Kitten pounces.

Oh-oh.

Kitten's in trouble!

Kitten runs out into the garden.

The sun is warm.

The birds are singing.

A butterfly flutters by.

Kitten pounces.

Oh-oh.

Kitten's in trouble!

Kitten pounces.

Kitten runs home.

Kitten yawns

and takes a bath.

Kitten
washes his face

and licks
his paws.

Kitten curls up
and goes to sleep.

Oh-oh!